50¢

Starry, Starry Night

Adapted by Bill Scollon
Based on the episode by Michael Rabb
Based on the series created by Chris Nee
Illustrated by Character Building Studio
and the Disney Storybook Art Team

DISNEY PRESS

New York • Los Angeles

First Edition
ISBN 978-1-4231-9419-4

G658-7729-4-14087

Manufactured in the USA
For more Disney Press fun, visit www.disneybooks.com

Doc McStuffins is excited.
Her brother, Donny, is excited, too.

They are going to watch a
meteor shower!

Doc tells Donny about meteors.
"Meteors are glowing rocks that
race across the sky."

Dad made star-shaped cookies.
"The cookies are star-tastic!"
Doc says.

Henry lives next door.
He has a new telescope.

Doc wants to see it. Hurry, Doc!
The meteor shower starts soon.

Henry shows Doc the telescope.
Oh, no! Everything looks blurry.

The telescope is broken.
Now Henry will not see the meteors.

Doc wants to fix the telescope.
Hurry, Doc! The meteor shower
starts soon.

Henry will wait with Donny.
"I'll be right back," says Doc.

The Doc is in!
Doc's toys come to life.

They say hello to the telescope.
Her name is Aurora.

Aurora cannot see well.
She thinks Lambie is a dog!

Doc knows what to do.
"Time for your checkup!" says Doc.

Doc shows Aurora a picture
of a whale.

Aurora thinks the whale
is a pretzel.

Doc knows what is wrong.
"Aurora has Blurry-star-itis!"
she says.

Glasses may help Aurora see better.

"I wear glasses," says Hallie.

"Oh, no!" Hallie says.

"My glasses are missing."

Hallie finds her glasses.
"Maybe Aurora is missing
something, too," Doc says.

Doc looks at Aurora's box.
Aurora is missing her eyepiece!

Aurora needs the eyepiece.
It will help her see well.

Doc thinks the eyepiece fell out.
It may be in Henry's yard.
"Road trip!" says Stuffy.

"Is the telescope fixed?" Henry asks.
"Almost," says Doc.

Hurry, Doc! The meteor shower
starts soon.

Doc looks for the eyepiece.
The eyepiece is in the grass.

Doc puts the eyepiece on Aurora.

Aurora looks at the sky.
She can see the stars.
She can see the moon.
The eyepiece works!

Doc gives Henry the telescope.
The telescope is fixed.
Thanks, Doc!

The meteor shower starts.
Meteors race across the sky.

Henry looks through his telescope.
He can see the meteors!

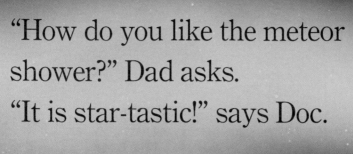

"How do you like the meteor shower?" Dad asks.
"It is star-tastic!" says Doc.